Dedication

To Enzo and Anna who inspire me each day. You are my world, my inspiration and my encouragement to keep coming up with more crazy stories to share with the world. Thank you to all the families who have welcomed me into their home to care for their most precious gift. Finally, thank you to iUniverse for helping make this book really come alive. Without any of you, *Fornax* would still be in hibernation begging to come alive.

Preface

If only I had a book like this to get me excited about brushing as child. Years later, as an adult, I became a nanny for families in the USA. To my surprise, those kids learned that I, too, nagged them about their teeth. This usually looked like me frantically running after them holding their toothbrushes for a late-night game of tag. That's when Fornax came to life and late-night tag games were replaced with a new adventure each night as we pretended to clean their playground. I have to say the slide (their tongue) was always the most fun to brush. I hope that you and your children, too, can replace your late night bickerings with a fun story like this one before they start to brush.

FORNAX, THE FRIENDLY TOOTHBRUSH AT THE PLAYGROUND!
AN ADVENTURE ABOUT MIA AND HER FRIENDLY TOOTHBRUSH, FORNAX.

iUniverse books may be ordered through booksellers or by contacting:

iUniverse
1663 Liberty Drive
Bloomington, IN 47403
www.iuniverse.com
844-349-9409

ISBN: 978-1-6632-4271-6 (sc)
ISBN: 978-1-6632-4272-3 (e)

Library of Congress Control Number: 2022914097

Print information available on the last page.

iUniverse rev. date: 09/16/2022

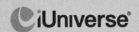

FORNAX, the FRIENDLY TOOTHBRUSH at the PLAYGROUND!

An adventure about Mia and
her friendly toothbrush, Fornax.

Author: Kaly Smith
Illustrator: the iUniverse team

"You know what, Mia, you just don't know how to have fun while brushing your teeth!"

Oh yeah?

Let me show you how much fun it can be to brush your teeth.

My mouth is like a playground, and my teeth are like a jungle gym, but who wants to play when it is all dirty? Later all the kids can come back and play when it is clean. Until then, it is going to be a bumpy ride...

What is the best way to clean a playground?

My way is to make it rain:

So ...

3

I rinse my mouth with nice warm water.

Then, it is time to clean my jungle gym – my teeth. That is a job for my toothbrush and a little bit of toothpaste. I have braces, too!

Hi, my name is Fornax the Friendly Toothbrush!

Meet Fornax, my friendly toothbrush. He helps me clean my jungle gym every day and lets me know when it is nice and clean.

So ...

We brush and brush my Rockwall until all the dirt — old food — comes out of those cracks between my teeth. Fornax and I agree that this will **definitely** make it easier for all the kids to climb through, up, down, under, and across.

The tops of my teeth are like monkey bars. That is what Fornax and I clean next.

So ...

We make sure that there is no jam – plaque – on each bar. That stuff builds up fast. You would not want kids to lose their grip and fall!

AAKK!

One child yells out, as he misses his grip while trying to hang onto my top tooth.

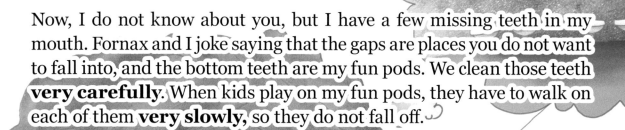

Now, I do not know about you, but I have a few missing teeth in my mouth. Fornax and I joke saying that the gaps are places you do not want to fall into, and the bottom teeth are my fun pods. We clean those teeth **very carefully**. When kids play on my fun pods, they have to walk on each of them **very slowly,** so they do not fall off.

Ha, ha, ha, a fun pod! AAAAAAHHH!

one child yells as he falls off because a squashed bean was left behind.

Now that the fun pods are sparkly clean, we move on to the slide. You have to keep it clean if you want to go fast!

Let's go, Fornax!

My tongue is like the slide. We polish it with a little toothpaste. Boy, those kids are going to have so much fun!

"Ahh, gross. An old pizza slice and a stinky pickle and a smelly beet, and is that a jelly bean?" One child yells, confused to see such things on his slide. Another child at the end of the slide gets up rubbing his bottom and says,

Now, I know what you are thinking...

What about a zipline?

What 8 year old would not want to play with a zipline?

Yes, I have a zipline, too. I like using blue floss as my zipline because it tastes so good. I use my zipline to clean between each structure and to get kids from one side of my playground to the other. Sometimes, before I get to floss, they even find small handles– bits of food Fornax and I missed – to help them go flying through the scented air.

"Look, Ann, a noodle that I found behind this tooth." A friend shouts out as she passes it to Zoe.

"This is going to be so much fun," Zoe says as she places the noodle on the zipline. Will then finds a left-behind piece of corn and says, **"Look! A piece of corn"**

LOOK! A piece of corn.

LOOK! Ann, a noodle that I found behind this tooth.

Now that Fornax and I showed you how much fun we have together, **I have one question...**

Can you play the same game that Fornax and I play when we brush my teeth?
Just remember ...
The front and back of your teeth will be your crazy rock wall.
The top teeth will be your fun monkey bars.
The bottom teeth will be your slippery fun pods.
The long tongue will be your fast slide.
And your floss will be the best zipline you will ever have.

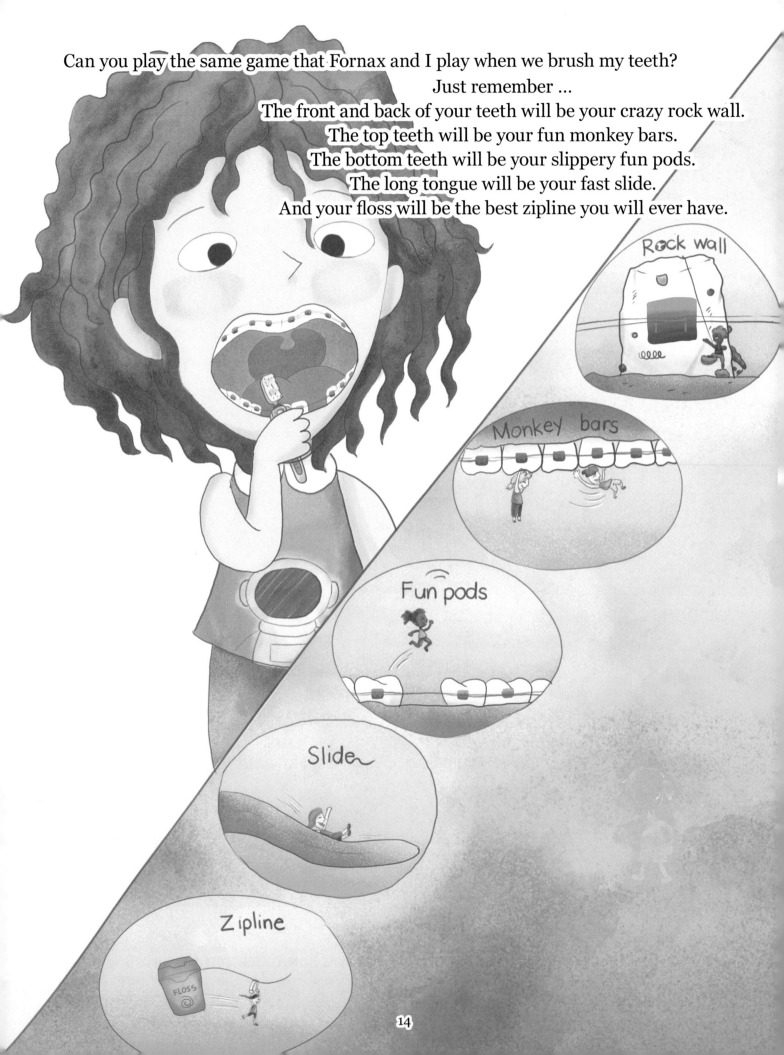

Rock wall

Monkey bars

Fun pods

Slide

Zipline

FLOSS

14

Feel free to use your own imagination when you brush. My friend
Sam tells everyone that it is a seesaw that gets brushed everyday.

Can you guess what that is?

OK, I will tell you. It is a loose tooth!

Now that Fornax and I are finished cleaning my playground, it is time for bed.

When I fall asleep, I hope to dream about all my friends and me having a blast playing on the cleanest, brightest, shiniest, safest, and coolest playground you will ever see – the playground created and kept clean by Fornax and me.

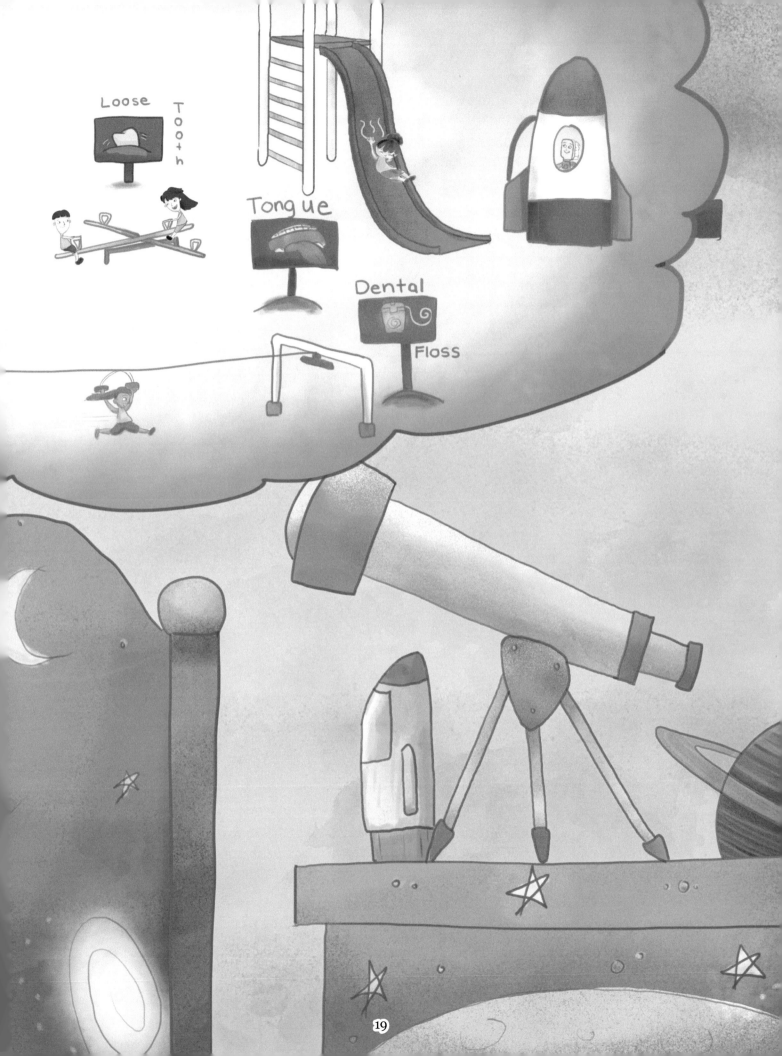

OUR PLAYGROUND RULES

1. Have fun!

2. No food or drinks while playing!

3. Do not play w/ ropes on playground!

~~The End~~

Read Again
In 5,4,3,2,1

What will you brush?

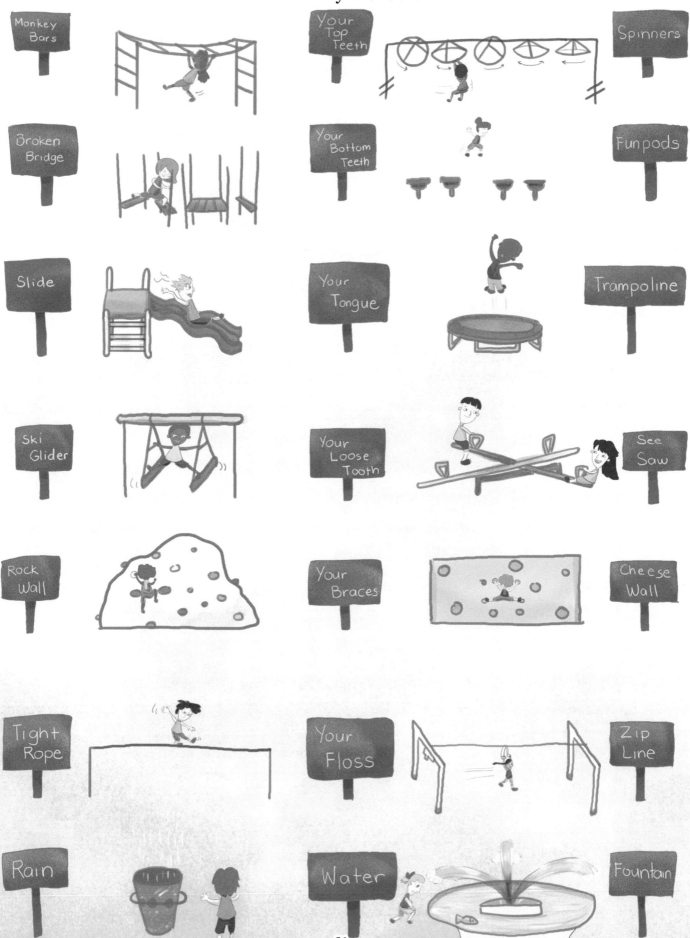

Monkey Bars	Your Top Teeth / Spinners
Broken Bridge	Your Bottom Teeth / Funpods
Slide	Your Tongue / Trampoline
Ski Glider	Your Loose Tooth / See Saw
Rock Wall	Your Braces / Cheese Wall
Tight Rope	Your Floss / Zip Line
Rain	Water / Fountain

KALY SMITH started a family in 2011 and moved from California to Michigan to start her next chapter.

She enjoys spending time with her two children. She loves creating stories for kids, companies, and schools. If she is asked the question, what has been her favorite job? Her answer would be A mother first and working as a nanny second. If you asked her why, she would say because kids inspire her. Being a nanny and becoming a mom is how she can create stories like this. Seeing children's faces light up when they hear a story, they love makes all this possible.

Printed in the United States
by Baker & Taylor Publisher Services